Mother's Mother's Day

Lorna Balian

Abingdon Press   Nashville

MOTHER'S MOTHER'S DAY

Copyright © 1982, by Lorna Balian
All Rights Reserved
2nd Printing 1984
Library of Congress Cataloging in Publication Data

Balian, Lorna.
  Mother's Mother's Day.
  Summary: Hazel the mouse goes to visit her mother on
Mother's Day, but finds she has gone to visit her mother.
  [1. Mice—Fiction.   2. Mother's Day—Fiction]
  I. Title.
  PZ7.B1978Mo   [E]   81-10988   AACR2

ISBN 0-687-37097-3

Manufactured in the United States of America

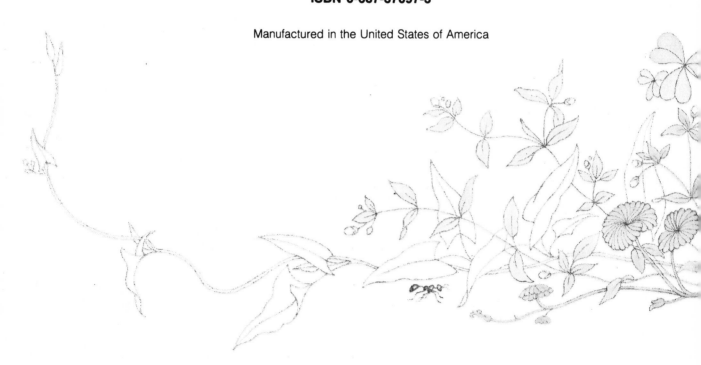

For Mary Ann

Hazel went to visit her mother.

It was a special day,

and she was taking her

a beautiful bouquet of violets.

But Mother wasn't home! Tsk!

Mother had gone to visit her mother.
Because it was such a special day,
she was taking her a big, plump acorn.

But Grandmother wasn't home! Tsk! Tsk!

Grandmother had gone to visit her mother.
Because it was such a very special day,
she was taking her a ripe, wild strawberry.

rype wyld

But Great-Grandmother wasn't home! Tsk! Tsk! Tsk!

Great-Grandmother had gone to visit her mother.
Because it was such a very, very special day,
she was taking her some kernels of popcorn.

But Great-Great-Grandmother wasn't home!

Tsk! Tsk! Tsk! Tsk!

Great-Great-Grandmother
had gone to visit her mother.
Because it was such a very, very, very special day,
she was taking her some soft feathers for her bed.

But Great-Great-Great-Grandmother was not home!

Great-Great-Great-Grandmother
had gone to visit Hazel.

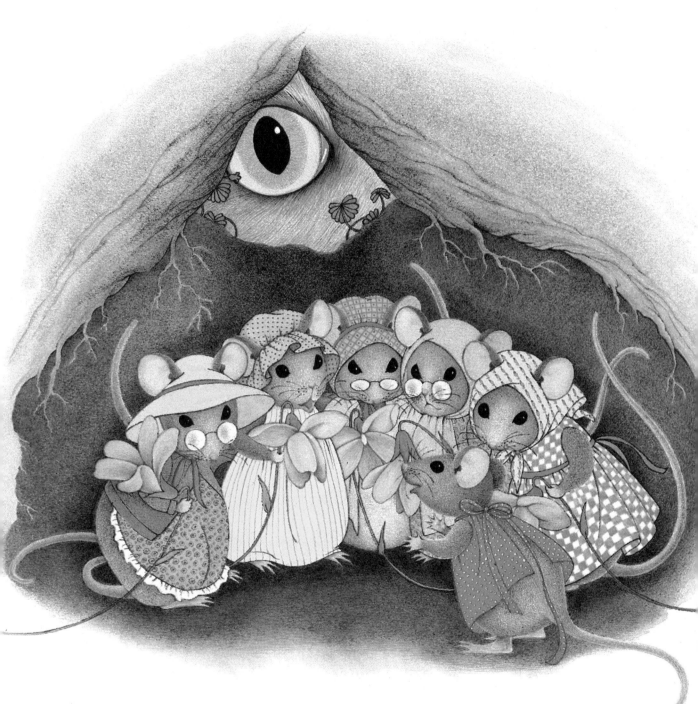

"Well, Happy Mother's Day, everyone!"
squeaked Hazel.

m a

10/0